Betty

the Polar Bear

Hannah R.S. Hayes

BETTY THE POLAR BEAR SERIES

BETTY THE POLAR BEAR
Copyright © 2013 by Hannah R. S. Hayes

ISBN: 978-1-77069-996-0

Word Alive Press
131 Cordite Road, Winnipeg, MB R3W 1S1
www.wordalivepress.ca

Library and Archives Canada Cataloguing in Publication

Hayes, Hannah R. S., 1987-, author
    Betty the polar bear / Hannah R.S. Hayes.

(Betty the polar bear series)
Short stories.
ISBN 978-1-77069-996-0 (pbk.)

    I. Title.

PS8615.A8393B47 2013   jC813'.6   C2013-902826-9

To my parents, Donald & Sandra Hayes,

who always instilled the importance of

reading and writing in me and helped

encourage my love of polar bears.

It was September 1st and summer was coming to an end; but for Betty, it didn't seem as though it was ending fast enough. Betty had an amazing summer with her family, but she hadn't seen any of her classmates since school ended. She really missed seeing all of them on a daily basis and was looking forward to being reunited. Betty had known them since kindergarten, and they had all been best friends ever since! There was Petunia the Peacock, Gilmar the Iguana, Marsalis the Monkey, Dover the Gopher and Isabelle the Giraffe. Each of them was quite different from the others, but yet somehow, they all got along extremely well and were the best of friends.

The first day of school had finally arrived and Betty was bouncing off of the walls! "Today! Today! Today!" she happily shouted as she jumped out of bed. She put on her favourite outfit, gobbled down her breakfast and waited by the door for the bus to pull up. Once it did Betty hopped on, where she was joyfully greeted by Petunia and Gilmar.

"BETTY!" they both happily exclaimed. "We missed you!"

"I missed you guys too!" said Betty, giving them both massive hugs.

It didn't take them long to start sharing their summer vacation stories, and before they knew it, they had arrived at school.

"Well, time to go in and start a whole new year!" said Petunia.

"You bet!" said Betty.

They quickly put their stuff in the lockers and then scurried off to their new classroom, where they were greeted by Mrs. Christie the Horse, their favourite teacher of all!

Soon after, Petunia, Gilmar and Betty were seated; Marsalis, Isabelle and Dover came in. Everyone was reunited at last, and no one was as excited as Betty to be back! That excitement unfortunately started to fade when this beautiful zebra entered the classroom. Mrs. Christie greeted the zebra with a friendly handshake and asked her to stay up at the front while she introduced her to the class. Betty became quite aware of all the whispers being said about this zebra.

"Ooooooohh look how beautiful her stripes are," said Gilmar.
"Have you ever seen such a gorgeous animal?!" said Petunia.
"Look at those eyes!" said Dover.

After hearing these comments being made about this zebra, Betty became quite jealous, and before even giving the zebra a chance, Betty had already made her mind up that she did not like her.

Mrs. Christie introduced the zebra to the class.

"Class, I'd like you to meet Zena. She just moved here from up north and is going to be a part of our class for the next year. Please help her to feel welcome and right at home."

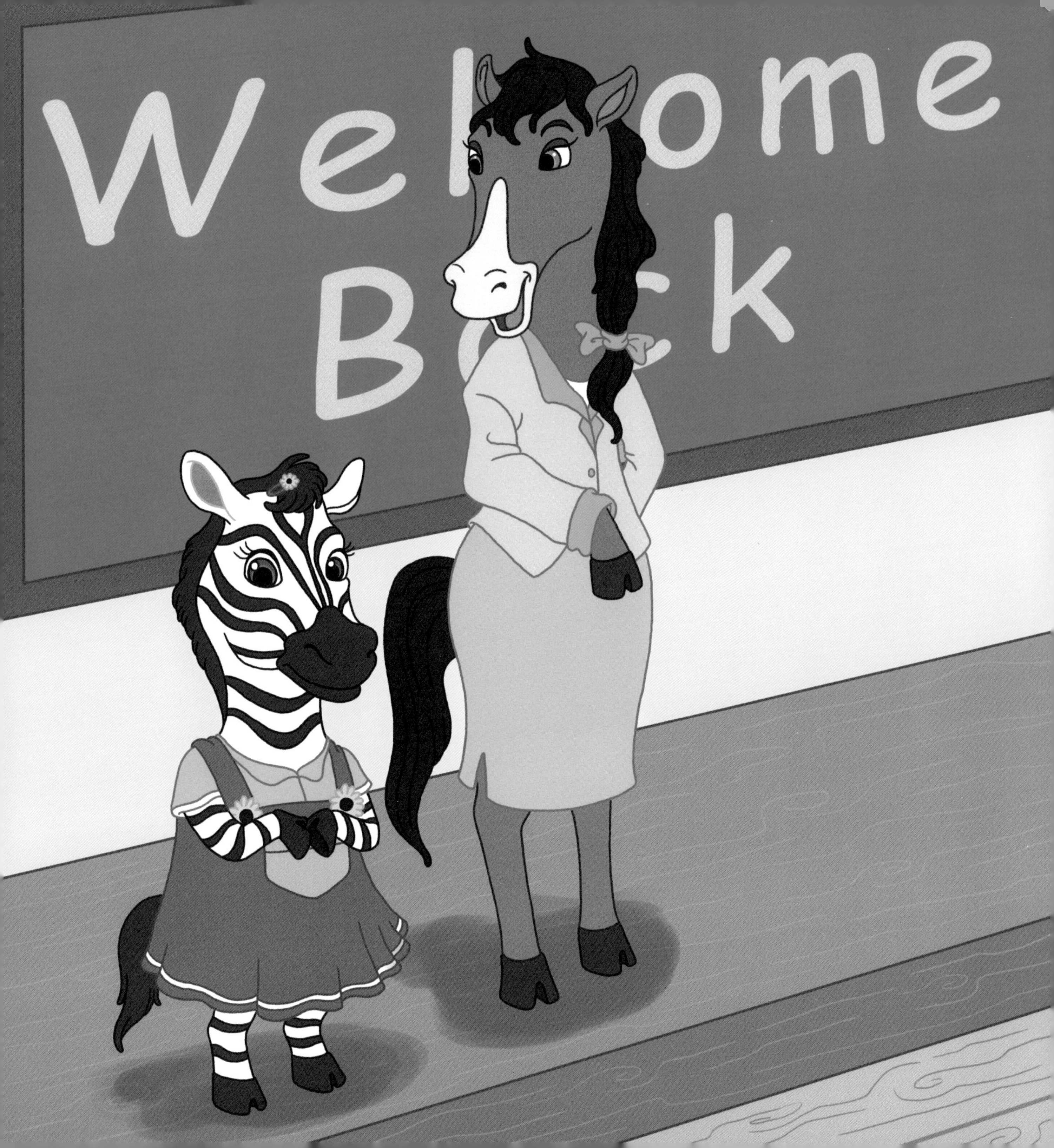
Wel ome
B ck

Without hesitation, all of Betty's friends jumped up out of their seats to introduce themselves to Zena and took an instant liking to her. Betty, however, became quite upset and annoyed that this new student was taking away all of the attention from her.

"Who does this Zena think she is?" said Betty to herself as she looked on in disgust.

After Zena was greeted by each classmate, she realized that Betty hadn't bothered to introduce herself. "Hi, I'm Zena. It's nice to meet you. What's your name?" said Zena, reaching out to shake Betty's hand.

Betty, however, did not appreciate Zena's friendliness and barely said anything back to her. Zena didn't take it personally and went to sit down. It didn't take long for Betty to start feeling ignored and no longer needed. All through class she struggled to hold back tears, and as time went on she kept feeling worse and worse about Zena.

an apple a day keeps the doctor away

Once lunch break came around, all of Betty's friends paid more attention to Zena than they did to her. Betty ended up sitting in the lunchroom all alone as she watched her so-called "friends" treat Zena like she was royalty or a celebrity. Betty held herself together for the rest of the day, but broke down once she got home.

When Betty entered her house, her mom was in the kitchen preparing dinner and heard the front door slam. Right away, Betty's mother knew something was wrong. She quickly came to see Betty, who had plopped down on the couch pouting with her arms crossed. Betty's mom sat down beside her and asked what was wrong.

"Betty, you were SO excited this morning when you left for school, and now you are extremely upset. What happened?"

Betty, on the brink of tears, said, "A zebra named Zena joined our class today and everyone was making such a big deal out of her and ignored me!"

"Ooooh I see," said Betty's mom. "I know that you're upset, but I'm sure your friends were just excited to have a new student join the class and they haven't forgotten about you!"

"YES THEY HAVE!" Betty insisted. "They don't care about me anymore! They'd rather be friends with this other creature! I just don't understand what makes her so much 'better' than me," Betty said in a blubbery tone.

In a very calm and loving way, Betty's mom put her arms around Betty and said, "Betty, God designed you just the way you are for a reason, and He designed Zena just the way she is. Nothing is wrong with either of you—in fact, you are both beautiful and unique in your own ways. There is no one else in this world who is like you, and wanting to be someone else is a waste of who you are."

Betty, still pouting, listened to what her mother had to say and started to think. "Hmm," said Betty. "I do have certain features that that zebra doesn't have and that she will never have—like my facial features."

"Betty," said her mom, "it's not about what you have and what Zena doesn't have. It's about embracing what God's given you and realizing that you are just as precious to Him as Zena is or any of your other friends."

Betty was starting to feel better and listened intently to what her mother had to say. "Look at your other friends, Betty. Marsalis, Dover, Petunia, Isabelle and Gilmar are all quite different, not only in their appearances but in their talents, personalities and several other ways. If we were all the same, this world would be a boring place," said Betty's mom.

"Yes, I guess you're right," said Betty as she stopped pouting and uncrossed her arms.

"Give her a chance, Betty. You never know, she might end up becoming one of your best friends," said her mom. "Remember when you didn't like Marsalis at first? You thought he was too silly? Now look at you guys!"

"Okay, Mom! I get it! I will give Zena a chance."

"Good. Now go wash up for dinner!"

Before Betty knew it, it was day two of the new school year. Betty woke up still feeling a little bit unsure about the whole Zena situation, but she reminded herself about what her mom said and decided to give Zena a fair chance.

The school bus arrived right on time, and Betty hopped on and headed for a seat. She was expecting to see her usual friends, but instead she found Zena, who was sitting alone. Betty hesitated, but then decided to go and sit down beside Zena.

"Hi, Zena!" said Betty in a friendly and welcoming tone.

With a surprised look on her face Zena responded with "Hi, Betty!"

"I wanted to apologize for how I acted yesterday," said Betty.

"Oh that's okay! I know that having a new student join the class can be difficult," said Zena.

"Even so, that still didn't justify my actions, and I want us to start over," said Betty.

"I'd like that too," said Zena with a smile.

Once the air was cleared between them, it didn't take long to find out that despite their different outward appearances, they had quite a bit in common.

"I think this is going to be a wonderful friendship!" said Betty with a big smile on her face.

"I agree!" said Zena.

CPSIA information can be obtained
at www.ICGtesting.com
Printed in the USA
LVIC06n0850051113
359700LV00004BA/13

* 9 7 8 1 7 7 0 6 9 9 9 6 0 *